Merry Christmas, Sean!

Love,

Aunt Y

&

Uncle Scott

For David Sohl, in memory of his father Kevin

The Scott Newman Center

Fundamental to the Scott Newman Center's philosophy is the prevention of substance abuse through education and the development of innovative, media-based programs targeting families, schools and communities. The Center, founded in 1980 by Paul Newman, is a non-profit organization located in southern California. Since its inception, the Center has maintained close ties to the entertainment community and has access to many of its resources. The organization also has partners in the academic community through its special relationship with the University of California. The unique combination of access to the world's largest pool of media resources and the most accurate and current research and evaluation data contributes much to the professional quality of the Center's projects and materials.

Commissioned jointly in 1993 by Roberts Rinehart Publishers and the Scott Newman Center, *Ordinary Splendors* is intended to affirm universal values in the words and stories from people throughout the globe. A portion of the sales proceeds will be dedicated to the good work of the Center.

For more information, contact:
The Scott Newman Center
6255 Sunset Boulevard, Suite 1906
Los Angeles, CA 90028-7420
1-800-783-6396

ORDINARY SPLENDORS

TALES OF VIRTUES AND WISDOMS

By Toni Knapp
Art by Kevin Sohl

Foreword by Joanne Woodward and Paul Newman

ROBERTS RINEHART PUBLISHERS

in cooperation with
The Scott Newman Center

Foreword

Folklore, as in art, turns the ordinary into the magical, gives beauty to the ways of man, and dignity to the joys of life. The folktales and art in this book bring together the spiritual and moral dimensions of common human experience—necessary building blocks for strong values and beliefs at a young age: responsibility, respect, honor, integrity. We hope the wisdoms and virtues depicted by these animal characters may help to create resilience in young readers—kids who will not succumb to the temptations that can undermine and destroy healthy lives. The proceeds of this book will help The Scott Newman Center to develop innovative drug education and prevention technologies for children and families.

Joanne Woodward

Paul Newman

Contents

ARION
AND THE DOLPHIN

A long time ago, a famous young poet and musician named Arion was sailing home from Italy to Greece, where he lived at the court of King Periander in Corinth. The voyage was long. He passed the time singing and playing his lyre, and watching the dolphins that raced alongside the ship's bow as if guiding it. Although he feared them, he watched them by the hour, hypnotized by their mystical beauty.

He could only imagine what they must be like, and he judged them by their appearance—strong, powerful bodies that could swim faster than his ship and leap high into the air in graceful, flashing curves. Sometimes Arion could see the rows of sharp teeth behind their smiles and he would shiver at the thought of being eaten by them. Still, from the safety of the deck, he could not resist their cheerfulness.

DOLPHIN

Fear and mistrust of the unknown keeps us from discovery and understanding. In this semi-legendary story from ancient Greece, a young boy learns that in all of nature, friendship has no boundaries and speaks the language of the heart.

ARION AND THE DOLPHIN

"They are very ordinary creatures," a sailor told him.

"They are very splendid," said Arion, and each day he played and sang just for them. He began to recognize some of the dolphins, especially one with an odd, round mark on its dorsal fin. Sometimes when the sun was just right, it glowed slightly pink, like a circle of light. Like a pearl. When Arion played, the dolphin seemed to jump higher and closer than the others, as if charmed by his music. And so he began to play just for her.

On the day land was sighted, Arion ran to the quarterdeck and looked out. In the distance was Greece and home! He lifted his lyre and began to play as never before. Then, on the last beautiful note, the ship lurched against the waves and Arion fell overboard.

Down, down he went as the water closed darkly around him. In his mind he screamed his panic: *No. No. I don't want to drown.*

But something was happening. He could feel it—a rushing motion as dolphins surrounded him. He could make out their smiles and sharp teeth as they bumped and pushed him with their beaks. Were they going to eat him? Terror filled his heart as the dolphins swam around him in swift circles.

Suddenly, he felt himself being lifted up . . . up . . . into the light and air! Held afloat by two dolphins, he drifted dreamily. He felt the warmth of their bodies and their delicate skin—not scales but skin—as they swam slowly and studied him with intelligent brown eyes. Now and then they blew out breaths of steam and made sounds that resembled whistles and clicks.

Arion dared to look at the dolphin on his right. She had been clicking for some time and was watching him curiously, smiling. She rocked in the water and brushed softly against him. Then she rocked over on her side, offering him her dorsal fin. At its center was the pink circle. She bobbed her head impatiently, waiting. Arion hesitated, then understood. He would have to trust. He grasped her fin with both hands and slipped onto her back. And with the other dolphins following behind, they soared with infinite grace through the sea to the familiar shore below the king's palace.

Arion stood waist-deep in the shallow water next to his dolphin and put his hand gently on her side. How could he say thank you or goodbye? She clicked softly, then turned and followed her pod out to sea.

Would anyone believe his story? When King Periander heard all that had

happened, he was dubious, of course. But he knew Arion could not have made it up, and soon the story of Arion and the dolphin spread throughout the country.

One day, Arion sat by the seashore, thinking about the dolphins and the utterly amazing wonder of their being. He was not of their world. He had fallen into it by mistake. And though knowing nothing about them, he had feared them. Yet when he needed help, they had saved him. He was alive because of them.

Never had he felt so incredibly sad. He picked up his lyre and began to play softly. From the distance, sweet warbling whistles mixed with clicks and squeaks floated over the water. The unmistakable voices of dolphins!

Almost instantly, Arion could see the curved dorsal fins rising above the waves. And finally, *his* dolphin—leaping joyfully as irridescent water poured off her dark back and creamy sides like liquid glass. Smiling. Inviting him to play. Behind her, the others frolicked and waited.

This time Arion was not afraid. Laughing and shouting, he pulled off his tunic and ran into the water to meet his friend—this wonderful ordinary splendor. ●

THE YOUNG CRAB AND HER MOTHER

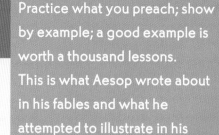

CRAB

Practice what you preach; show by example; a good example is worth a thousand lessons. This is what Aesop wrote about in his fables and what he attempted to illustrate in his simple tales told by animals.

In a small, rocky tidal pool by the edge of the sea, lived a charming family of crabs. Their shells were soft yellow with lovely purple spots that blended well with the rocks and water.

The youngest crab was mottled with different shades of blue and green and pink. "That's because you spend too much time in the sun," admonished her mother who had just had a long nap on a sunny rock.

"But I've just been sitting next to you," said the little crab.

One evening just after sunset, the family went for a stroll on the amber sand above the high-tide line. "I want everyone to be cheerful and have a good time," snapped mother crab.

"Then why are you so crabby?" asked the little crab, shuffling along.

Mother crab kept watchful eyes on her little one as she scurried to keep up. "Why don't you learn to walk straight?" she scolded, waving a claw. "You shuffle backwards and sideways with every step you take."

"I'm walking just like you do," the little crab piped up as her mother came scuffling sideways toward her.

"Of course you are," said mother crab, feeling very foolish. "There's no better way to walk. Thank you for reminding me."

So the little family of crabs danced along the shore—to the left to the right, backwards and forwards—a little crustacean chorus line led by mother crab. Forever after, she set a good example. ●

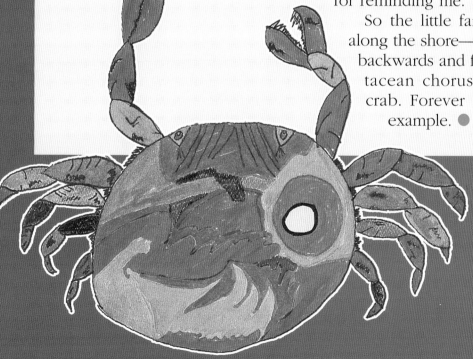

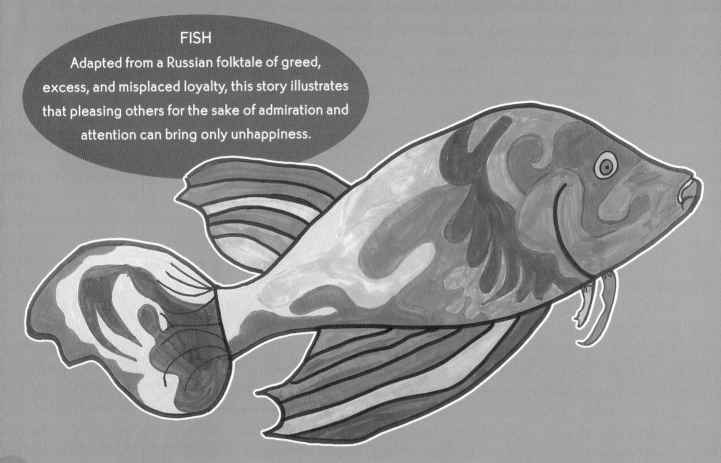

FISH

Adapted from a Russian folktale of greed, excess, and misplaced loyalty, this story illustrates that pleasing others for the sake of admiration and attention can bring only unhappiness.

THE RAINBOW FISH

The young boy sat by a deep, quiet pool in the river and threw out his line. He had not caught any fish all afternoon, and he wanted so much to please his father. It was rare to go home without a catch, but if it happened, he would simply repeat what everyone else said at such times: "Oh, I caught the Rainbow Fish, but it got away." There was, after all, no such thing as a Rainbow Fish.

The boy held the rod and listened to the gently rushing water, wishing his father were there, and knowing he was too busy. The sun was low in the sky, and shadows crossed the river and spread under the trees. Suddenly, the line tightened and began to pull downstream. His heart pounding, the boy jumped to his feet and reeled the line in until the water churned and boiled at his feet. There, floating at the surface, was a fish more beautiful than any he could imagine. Its billowing tail fanned the water like blue silk, its fins were delicate clouds of jade, and its body radiated colors like stained glass.

Hardly daring to breathe, the boy knelt down on the bank. His hands floated under the fish without a ripple. Gently he removed the hook from its mouth and slid the fish back into the water. For a

THE RAINBOW FISH

moment, the fish tested its freedom, but instead of swimming away it looked up and spoke. "I am the Rainbow Fish. You saved my life. If you ever need anything, just come here and call me." Then it disappeared.

Stunned and amazed, the boy gathered up his things and hurried home. "Did you catch anything?" his father asked without much interest.

"Oh, yes. I caught the Rainbow Fish, but it was so beautiful I let it go." Everyone in the family laughed, but the boy insisted it was true.

"Well, why didn't you ask for a reward?" his older brother taunted rudely. "Go back and tell it we need a new truck."

To prove that he had told the truth, the boy went to the river and called the beautiful Rainbow Fish. He worried. What if it didn't come? What if he had imagined it all? Suddenly, there it was, and the boy told it what had happened. "Your wish is granted," the fish said kindly.

The boy ran all the way home and saw his family staring with open mouths at a big, shiny, new truck. A few days later, his mother told him to go fishing again. "And if you see your fishy friend, ask it for a bigger house."

Not wanting to offend his mother, the boy went to the river and again called the Rainbow Fish. The day was cool and cloudy and the river was moving very fast. Finally, the fish appeared and the boy told him what his mother wanted. "Her wish is granted," it said.

When the boy got home, his small, comfortable house had turned into a mansion with white pillars and flower gardens. From that day, his family sent him to ask the magic fish for more and more—clothes, jewels, servants. Each request was granted, but nothing made them happy. And they were so busy making wish lists, they ignored the one person who was making it all possible.

One day, his father announced he wanted to own the river. Wanting desperately to please his father, the horrified boy ran to the river. It was almost dark and the wind blew and the water roared. "Oh kind and beautiful Rainbow Fish," he called loudly, "please come to me. I need you."

Hidden in shadows behind the trees, his father watched and listened as the fish appeared bouncing on the waves. "What is it this time?" it demanded impatiently.

Tears ran down the boy's face. "My father wants to own the river. What

THE RAINBOW FISH

should I do?"

"I have given you all that you asked of me, and you're still not happy. Why?" asked the fish.

"I didn't want all those things," the boy answered. "I only wanted my father to think I was worthwhile."

"You let everyone take advantage of you for the sake of false admiration. Now, what do *you* really want?" the fish asked gently.

"For everything to be the way it was, only better."

"Granted," said the Rainbow Fish. It leaped in an arc of brilliant colors and disappeared in the river.

The boy turned and saw his father. Sadness was in his eyes and on his face. Not knowing what to say, they walked quietly home through the woods, and there was their old house—comforting, welcoming and familiar.

"What happened to our house?" yelled his brother. "Go tell your fish we want it back."

The boy looked at him and smiled. "If you want a big house, then you will have to figure out how to get one."

The next day, he and his father went fishing. They talked for a very long time about important things. And when his father hugged him tight, a flash of color lit the water. ●

THE LITTLE BLOND SHARK

The little blond shark, Ka-ehu-iki, had never gone beyond his deep-sea home near Panau. One day, he asked his parents for permission to explore the wide ocean world he lived in. His goal was to meet the fierce and noble King of All the Sharks. "You will meet many creatures along the way," they told him. "Be very careful of the company you choose."

After many days of travel, the little shark felt lonely and sometimes afraid. He happened to come to the cave of the Shark King of Hilo, who asked him, "Why do you travel here?"

Shaking with fright, the little shark said, "For pleasure and to learn about the world. Would you, my lord and chief, add dignity to my journey and be my companion along the way?"

So pleased was the king by the young shark's respectful and disarming manner, that he agreed. And as they journeyed on to Kau, Kona, Kohala and Hamakua, the little blond shark persuaded each of the Shark Kings to travel with him. And so it was that the little blond shark traveled in the company of kings. He felt very safe.

They traveled in peace until they came to the domain of the Shark King of Hana. "We must be careful," said one of the kings. "He and his ruffian guards like to fight, and will not let us pass."

"My good kings, surely they will not harm us if I indicate our friendship," said the innocent little shark. Immediately, a giant guard appeared and swam around him in a threatening way. Little Blond Shark explained politely that they were on a pleasure trip, and meant no harm. So surprised was the guard by the tiny shark's confidence that he forgot what he was supposed to do.

But the hostile king shark was ready.

SHARK

Maintaining courage, dignity and self-reliance while navigating life's turbulent waters is illustrated in this charming parable from Hawaii.

THE LITTLE BLOND SHARK

"How dare you come into my territory?" he roared. Without warning, he charged with open jaws and gleaming teeth. Fearlessly, Little Blond Shark grabbed the king's fins and held on while the giant thrashed and fought to dislodge him. Finally, worn out and humiliated, the king swam away in defeat.

The astonished Shark Kings gathered around their little friend and praised him for his courage. The guards were so happy to be free of their cruel master that they begged to join the royal party and provide safety along the way. And so it was that Little Blond Shark arrived at the cave of the King of All the Sharks in the company of kings and a fleet of guardian sharks.

They sent a respectful message to inform their noble monarch that they were on a peaceful sightseeing tour, and asked permission to pay him homage. When he appeared before them, they were awed. He was enormous and very old, covered with barnacles and draped in sea moss. Yet his body radiated colors like jeweled prisms. Shaking, Little Blond Shark found his voice and introduced each of the shark kings by name and kingship, and explained the reason for his journey.

"How is it that a little yellow shark travels with kings?" the great ruler asked. All the shark kings answered at once and explained all that had taken place. The great king was so pleased by the little shark's dignity and courage that he adopted him as his prince. "I grant you power second to none in this broad ocean. You will always have safe passage through all the royal domains."

And so it was that the little blond shark returned home in the company of kings, a fleet of guardian sharks and a royal pilot shark. His father welcomed them with joy and pride. "You chose your friends well, my son."

"No," said the Shark King of Hilo. "He earned our respect and friendship with his honesty and goodness." ●

THE GIRAFFE'S LONG NECK

The young giraffe was lovely to behold. Her long, graceful neck stretched above her sloping body and impossibly long and delicate legs. Soft, smoky eyes looked out from under the little knobs on top of her head.

"Look at this neck and these legs," she moaned in despair. "Why can't I be like other animals? I'm tired of the altitude. And I'll never be a dancer! I can't even lie down!"

Her grandfather listened quietly. He was a kind chief, wise in the ways of solving problems. "Let me tell you about the time when we *were* like all the other land animals." And so he began.

Once giraffe looked much like the antelope—the kudu and the eland. Our legs and necks were much shorter. We ate from the ground and were always looking down for food. Well, there came a great drought—the grass and bushes dried up and so did most waterholes. There was nothing to eat or drink. Dust devils whirled and the horizon shimmered in the terrible heat.

GIRAFFE
Adapted from an East African and an ancient Bushman legend. About the perils of vanity, the value of inner beauty, and the potential for transformation in all of us.

THE GIRAFFE'S LONG NECK

One day, Giraffe and his good friend Rhino walked on the scorched plains in search of food. "We're going to starve," said Rhino.

Giraffe was looking up at the tree tops. "Look at all those tender green leaves and fruit. If only we could reach them."

"Grrmph!" grumbled Rhino, spitting out a dry twig, and squinting at the trees. "Maybe the Magician Man can help us. He's very powerful and wise."

Giraffe agreed, and they set off across the dry savannah to the hut of the great Magician, who actually was the god of land animals. He smiled, and listened to their story.

"Of course I will help you. I forgot to make any animals tall enough to reach the treetops. Come back tomorrow at exactly noon and I will give you magic herbs to eat. But don't be late."

Giraffe and Rhino went home to wait for the night to pass. The next morning at sunrise, Giraffe trotted off. "Don't be late," she reminded Rhino. At exactly noon, Giraffe and the Magician waited for Rhino. After several minutes, the impatient Magician gave all the magic herbs to Giraffe, and immediately she began to grow taller. By the time Rhino arrived, it was too late. Giraffe was already nibbling happily from the trees.

Grandfather paused for a moment in his story.

"But I want to run like the wind, not just eat leaves all day," the young giraffe complained to her grandfather.

"Let me finish," he said patiently, and continued his story.

Not long after the magic herbs did their job, a great fire raged across the grasslands and all the animals stampeded in panic. No one would stop to help the oxbirds trapped in a tree. Then the giraffe came galloping by. She saw the nest and the birds, snatched them from the tree and ran like the wind ahead of the flames, her head and neck safely above the smoke.

"No one else was tall enough to save them?" asked the little giraffe.

"No one but Giraffe," answered Grandfather, "who is beautiful to behold and runs like the wind. So will you."

And she did. "Oh, just look at these legs and this neck," she sang, floating over the ground, draped in morning mist and evening moonlight, her most beautiful neck gracing the heights.

She passed a rhino browsing for berries. "Grrmph!" he grumbled, on seeing her loveliness. ▪

THE PRINCE AND THE RHINOCEROS

Once upon a time in India, a rare white rhinoceros was born. It was given to a noble prince who was very lonely and whose kingdom was poor. The prince was so delighted with the unusual gift that he laughed joyfully. So, of course, he named the little calf Great Joy.

The prince treated the rhino with great kindness. He fed him rice, fruit and choice tender plants, and he always spoke in a kind and gentle voice. Great Joy grew and was happy. The prince visited him often, and the calf would charge joyfully toward him whenever he spoke.

The prince thought Great Joy was quite beautiful. At sunrise, he would be golden. At midday, the heat would surround him in pale waves. At sunset, he would be a canvas of pink and red and orange, and later the dark blue of evening. Sometimes after a rain, he would reflect everything around him. He seemed almost enchanted. "You are wonderful and special to me," the prince whispered softly.

RHINOCEROS

Harsh words are like knives to the soul. To speak unkindly and with anger brings unhappiness to others as well as to ourselves, as illustrated in this story from India's Jataka Tales, fables from the Buddha.

THE PRINCE AND THE RHINOCEROS

In time, Great Joy grew into an enormous bull with fine horns. He was very strong. One day he thought about his good life with the prince, and what he could give him in return. "I am only a rhino, but I can use my strength to help him earn gold for his kingdom."

He suggested to the prince that he compete in a contest of strength against the town's strongest bulls. The prince thought this would be a cheerful and entertaining pastime, and show the people how splendid was his rhino.

A rich merchant with many fine oxen agreed to the wager: Great Joy would pull a hundred loaded wagons usually pulled by his team of eight oxen. The bet was one thousand gold pieces.

The next day, the prince inspected the wagons and harnessed Great Joy to the front. Then he climbed onto the driver's seat. Great Joy waited for a few kind words of encouragement before starting. Instead, the prince waved a whip in the air and shouted, "Pull, you big wretch. Move, you worthless rhino."

Great Joy was shocked at his beloved prince's words. Wretch? Worthless? "I'm no wretch," he thought. "I'm not worthless, either." He stiffened his huge legs and refused to move an inch.

The prince was so humiliated that he ran home and hid in his royal bed. "I'm ruined," he cried.

Great Joy was filled with pain and sorrow. He needed to understand what he had done to deserve such cruel insults. After many days and nights without food or sleep, he went to the prince's shabby palace. "Oh, Prince, in all our years together have I ever done anything to hurt you?"

"No, never."

"Then why did you say those terrible things to me? Did you think my friendship and my strength were not enough to win? Was the thought of gold worth more than what I can offer?"

The prince hung his head. Tears ran down his face. "The gold blinded me. I forgot the importance of our friendship. I am so ashamed."

"Then we will try again," said Great Joy. "Go back to the merchant and double your bet."

Again the carts were loaded and Great Joy was harnessed to the front. The prince climbed up and sang out, "All right, you marvelous marvel, you splendid rhino, my Great Joy. It's up to you!"

THE PRINCE AND THE RHINOCEROS

The powerful rhino snorted, pawed the ground, and charged forward. His sides heaved as he pulled, until the last cart crossed the finish line. The townspeople cheered wildly as they covered him with garlands of flowers and strands of tinkling bells, and ribbons around his fine horn.

The prince collected his two thousand pieces of gold, then humbly thanked Great Joy for a job well done. That very evening, the prince and the rhino walked along the river in the red glow of sunset. "I didn't mean to say such hurtful words to you," the prince whispered. "Please forgive me."

"I already have," said Great Joy.

And that's how they lived forever after—in friendship and great joy. Never an unkind word passed between them. ▐

THE ELEPHANT PUZZLE

Once, if you can imagine, there were six children who had never seen an elephant. They had all heard stories about what elephants could do, but they could only imagine what an elephant actually looked like. Yet all of them were convinced that what each of them believed was absolutely true.

They argued constantly, day and night. They argued among themselves and with anyone who cared to listen. They fussed and yelled and sometimes jumped up and down to make a point. Their parents and teachers finally decided the children needed to learn the truth about elephants, and maybe something about themselves, too.

Plans were made to visit a wild animal park where some elephants lived. But the children had to agree to one thing: they would wear blindfolds at first to find out how close they were to the truth. So each of them, with eyes covered and excited beyond belief, approached a gentle elephant standing quietly in the shade.

The first child stepped nervously forward. He stood on tiptoe and ran his hands over the animal's huge side. "This

16

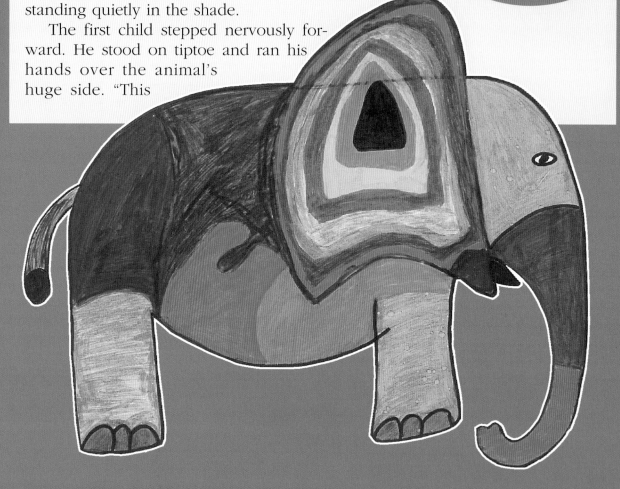

THE ELEPHANT PUZZLE

elephant is like a high, solid wall," he said, "and it's covered with warm, wrinkled leather."

The second child happened to bump against its tusk. "Ouch!" she said. Then she ran her hands along its smooth, cool roundness, down to the sharp pointed end. "Why would you think it's like a wall, when it's actually more like a spear?"

The third child, holding his breath and stretching out his arms, tried to reach around the animal's gigantic leg. "You're both wrong," he said. "This elephant is exactly like the huge tree in our yard, and it's probably green."

"Does it have leaves?" someone sneered, and everyone laughed.

The fourth child jumped up and down to reach the top of the elephant, and touched its enormous ear. It waved gently and cooled her warm face. "All of you are wrong," she announced. "This elephant is like a fan, and I'm sure it's yellow and red."

The fifth child had been listening quietly at the animal's other end. Its tail twitched back and forth and tickled his chin. "This elephant is like a strong rope," he said, and tried to swing on it.

Can you imagine the patience of this wonderful animal? Well, by now it was getting bored and restless, and playfully reached out its long trunk toward the sixth child. First, it touched her shoulder and then her back. It moved up her arm to her head and smelled her hair. Suddenly, the frightened girl grabbed it in her hands and screamed. "A snake! This is a giant snake!"

All the children began talking at once about their discoveries. At last it was time to find out who was right. One by one, each of them was lifted high onto the elephant's back, centered

> in front of the rope,
> behind the spear, the snake and the fan,
> at the top of the wall
> and above the trees.

They pulled off their blindfolds and could hardly believe what they saw—the amazing elephant in all its majesty. Then, one by one, they rode down to the ground on its wonderful trunk.

THE ELEPHANT PUZZLE

What happened then? Well, they looked up at the marvelous animal, and after a quiet minute they began to giggle, and then to laugh. "A wall. A tree. A rope!" howled the boys.

"A spear. A fan. A snake!" screamed the girls.

"Oh, we were so wrong," a boy said.

"But we were also right," a girl answered.

So they were. And forever after they learned as much as possible before forming opinions. ▮

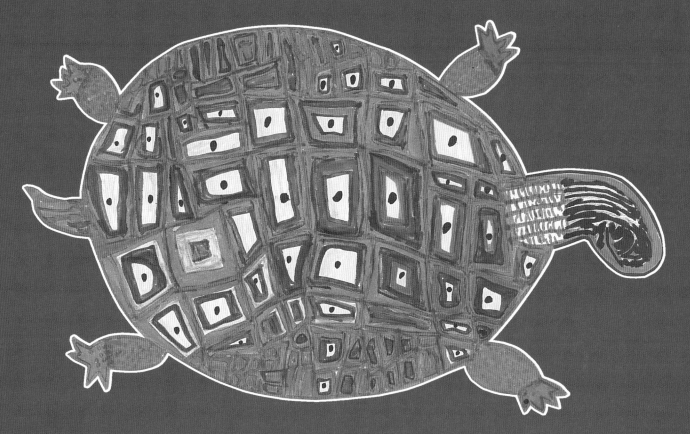

THE TORTOISE AND THE HARE

A handsome brown hare with strong legs and wonderful long ears was on his way to the river. He was the fastest hare in the west. He was *so* fast that no one ever bothered to race him. One morning as he sprang in and out of the tall grass, he saw a big rock up ahead. What wonderful colors and patterns it had, he thought—like a painting.

When he got closer, the rock was moving ever so slowly in the same direction. It was a tortoise! "I can't stop now," she said, "or I won't get to the river before dark."

"How long have you been walking?" asked Hare.

"Days and days," answered Tortoise.

"I'm going to the river too," Hare said. "I'd enjoy your company, but we don't move at the same speed. If you were a hare, I'd challenge you to a race."

TORTOISE

The tortoise as a symbol of perseverance appears in folklore around the world. This version of Aesop's best-loved fable illustrates the importance of staying focused on one's goals.

THE TORTOISE AND THE HARE

"Well, why not?" answered Tortoise. "It'll give me something to think about besides how heavy my shell is."

Hare was a little arrogant about his running speed. "But there's no way you can win," he said.

"Who knows?" said Tortoise. She started off, parting the grass as she went.

The hare watched in disbelief, and feeling a little guilty about his great speed, he made it a point of honor to start late. He nibbled some grass, sniffed the wind, then leaped ahead to find Tortoise. "I've admired your shell," he said as she plodded along, "It's very different."

"I had to dress it up for a festival, and I can't wait to wash it off," she explained without slowing down.

The hare then offered to wash her shell if she won. If she lost, which of course she would, she could brush his fur.

Tortoise agreed and kept on walking. "I heard a story once about a race between a rabbit and a turtle, but I can't remember how it went. Have you heard it?"

"No," said Hare. "Well, see you at the river," and he hopped away. Soon, he was so far ahead he stopped to rest.

Tortoise plowed over the warm ground, her neck stretched out in front. Now and then as she walked, she would grab a leafy plant with her beak and munch along the way. She moved her short legs in a steady rhythm, to-and-fro, to-and-fro, keeping the river in her mind's eye and imagining its cool ripples.

In the meantime, Hare met his friend the hedgehog, and they visited long into the afternoon. They talked about Hare's race with Tortoise.

"Shouldn't you be out there racing?" asked Hedgehog. "I heard a story once about a race like this. I think the turtle won."

"Don't be silly. That's not possible," said Hare, hopping off. Soon clouds moved overhead and a gentle rain fell softly. Tortoise loved the rain and kept on walking, but Hare took cover under some shrubs and fell asleep. When he woke, the sky had cleared and the sun was sinking slowly in the distance. "Oh, no!" he yelled, springing up on his big feet. "I'd better hurry." He leaped ahead, eating up the countryside with long strides, and looking for Tortoise in every direction. There was no sign of her. She had probably

given up and parked somewhere, he thought.

Soon there was no mistaking the sound of rushing water, and the sweetness of damp earth and perfumed flowers. Hare hopped to the river's edge near a brown rock that was half in the water.

"What took you so long?" asked the rock as a head popped out and four legs appeared.

"How did you get here?" asked Hare, surprised and annoyed.

"I walked," said Tortoise, pulling herself ashore.

"But this isn't possible," sputtered Hare. "I'm faster."

"If you wanted to win the race, you should have stayed in it. Now, please, I believe you agreed to wash my back."

The hare kept his word, but he never again agreed to race a tortoise. ▦

KING BRUCE AND THE SPIDER

The young king was tall and strong, with burnished hair and eyes the dark gray of the sea. His fair skin was bruised and caked with dirt after fighting and losing another battle against England. Now he was hiding like a coward in this small hut with a drooping roof and crooked door.

There were no windows, but fading afternoon light filtered through a hole in the roof and settled in the corners of the room. The king built

SPIDER

Legends and myths about the amazing spider and its enchanting webs have been spun around the world and appear in nearly every culture. This one from Scotland is thought to be mostly true. A long time ago in the year 1314, a small spider taught a king the importance of never giving up, and trying again when all seemed hopeless.

KING BRUCE AND THE SPIDER

a small fire to warm himself, then he stood and accidentally bumped against the ceiling rafter. Suddenly, a little gray spider ran across her torn web.

"Oh, no!" the king exclaimed. "My apologies. I didn't see your web." He bowed. "I am Robert Bruce, King of Scotland. Well, I *was* the king."

The spider scuttered into a shadowed corner.

"Don't be afraid. I won't hurt you," said the king.

The spider crept from her cranny and the king spoke. "I know you can't understand what I'm saying, but you should know that I'm hiding here because I lost six battles to save my country from the English. My army is gone, and I am alone." He took off his helmet, and ran his fingers over the royal circle of gold. "Can you fix your web?" he asked the spider.

Almost as an answer, the small spider began her work. She struggled to spin a silk thread across the space between the two rafters, but it was too short.

The king watched as the little spider threw another line of silk and missed again. All the while, he talked to her about his country, his army and his lost battles. He ran his hand over his tired face. "Oh, how I wish I was at home with my dog to comfort me. Instead, I'm in a hut talking to a spider."

The spider stopped her work as if listening. Then she turned and for the third time spun a thread and missed the rafter. The king glanced up at her. How brave she was. He began to cheer for her. He wanted her to succeed and save her web.

He blew on the fire and pulled an oatcake out of his knapsack. "Would you share a king's supper?" he asked the spider. "It's all I have left."

The spider stopped for a moment, as if thinking about it. Then she cast another thread and missed again. The king jumped to his feet. "Why do you keep trying? There's nothing I can do to help you." He felt sad and angry and sorry for the spider, and himself.

She answered by spinning another thread, and this time it caught. But as she scurried across, it broke and the tiny spider swung in midair.

The king clenched his fists as he watched. "Are you trying to tell me something? Did *I* give up too easily?"

The tiny spider ignored him and tried again. For the sixth time, she

KING BRUCE AND THE SPIDER

failed. "Don't you know when to give up?" the king shouted. Frightened, the spider scurried into the shadows.

"Yes. Hide," the king told her. "If an army of strong men and a king can run away, so can you." Minutes passed . . . where was she?

Finally, the spider ran out from the dark corner and balanced on the edge of the beam. The king held his breath. They were even now—they had both failed six times. "Try again, my friend," he said softly. "If you succeed this time, I promise to try once more."

The spider spun. The silk sailed out. It seemed to stop midair. Then, it wrapped around the wooden beam, and the little spider quickly ran across. She went right to work repairing her web.

The king let out his breath and smiled. "Well done, little friend." He watched her work long into the night until the fire went out. Morning came soon after and filled the dark hut with soft, pink light. And there, sparkling like a jewel, was the spider's new web—complete and perfect—with the spider resting in the center.

"My humble thanks," said the king, bowing. "Now I must keep my promise." He put on his helmet and cape. "One day I will tell my kingdom why I really tried one more time to reclaim my country." He smiled. "But no one will believe me."

King Robert Bruce succeeded on the seventh try, and freed Scotland from English rule. Whenever he saw a spider's web, he saluted in gratitude. ▪

THE GRASSHOPPER, THE MOUSE, THE BEE AND THE HARP

GRASSHOPPER

The grasshopper appears in fable and folklore from Africa to Aesop. Most often he is shown singing and dancing while everyone else is working! In this charming fairytale from Ireland about the power of laughter, Grasshopper saves the day *and* gets the last laugh.

Once on a small farm in very old Ireland, lived a widow and her son, Jack. Their crops had failed. They had no money, no food, and only the milk from their three cows kept them going. They had not laughed for a very long time.

One morning, Jack's mother decided they would have to sell one of their beloved cows. "Take her to the fair and sell her, and do it quickly before I change my mind."

When Jack got to the fair, a crowd was gathered around a mysterious little man with a mouse, a grasshopper, and a bee with a tiny harp. He put them on the ground and whistled and the most amazing thing happened: the bee

THE GRASSHOPPER, THE MOUSE, THE BEE, AND THE HARP

strummed the harp, and the mouse and grasshopper stood up and danced together.

Everyone at the fair began to laugh. They slapped their knees, wiped their eyes and fell against each other. Then they started dancing, too. They jumped and jigged and so did everything else—pots and pans, wheels and reels, dogs and cats, wagons and fenceposts. Even Jack and his cow. The town had never been in such a state.

When the grasshopper suddenly stopped dancing and started singing instead, the man put the little band into his pocket. Everything stopped as quickly as it had started, and all was quiet and still. As Jack stood leaning against his cow, the mysterious man asked him if he would like to own part of the band.

"Oh, yes," said Jack, "but I have no money and must sell my cow to help my poor mother."

The man smiled and reached into his pocket. "I will trade the bee and the harp for your cow. Your mother will laugh and your lives will be the better for it."

When Jack told his mother what he had done, she couldn't believe her ears. "You did *what?*" she screamed. Right away, the bee plucked the harpstrings and buzzed a tune. In a flash, Jack's mother began to giggle and laugh, clap her hands and tap her feet. Even the pots and pans, tables and chairs, the house, the barn and the two cows jumped, jigged, whirled and bounced. Jack couldn't believe his eyes.

He couldn't believe his mother, either, when she sent him back to the fair with their second cow. Naturally, when he heard the merriment and laughter again, he traded his cow for the mouse. And the following day, forgetting all about food or money, he traded his last cow for the grasshopper. "Watch out for him," the mysterious man said. "He loves to sing, but I don't let him because his voice is terrible. That's why he looks mad."

The little band was together again, and oh, how they all danced and laughed and hopped and jigged—Jack and his mother, the pots and pans, the house and the empty barn. And oh, how furious was Jack's mother when calm was restored. "We're ruined," she wailed.

"But you've laughed again," offered Jack.

"Laughter doesn't put food on the table," she cried.

THE GRASSHOPPER, THE MOUSE, THE BEE, AND THE HARP

But it did something for the soul, Jack thought. He went outside to think, and walked sadly down the road. A neighbor walking with her sheep called out to him. "Why aren't you out trying to win the hand of the king's daughter?" she asked cheerfully.

"What do you mean?"

"Don't you know? The princess hasn't laughed in seven years. The king has promised to give her in marriage to any man who can make her laugh three times. He must be desperate, poor fellow."

Jack ran all the way back to his farm, gathered up his little band and said goodbye to his mother. "I'm off to make our fortune."

At the royal castle, the king's guard warned Jack that if he failed to make the princess laugh, terrible things would happen to him. But Jack felt suddenly very brave as word went through the castle that he had come to win the hand of the princess.

He marched in with his little animals, all of them holding onto his shoelaces so as not to get lost. When the king and queen and the royal court saw Jack in his dusty, ragged clothes leading his strange little band, a roar of laughter filled the castle. And when the princess saw the ridiculous sight, she let out a laugh that caused her crown to fall off.

Only two laughs to go, thought Jack. He bowed to the princess, called his little animals to attention, and whistled. The bee plucked the harp as never before, and the mouse and grasshopper grabbed hold of each other and spun into a splendid waltz. Naturally, the king grabbed the queen and did the same, and so did the entire court. The castle itself and everything in it began to hop and jig, and miracle of miracles, the princess laughed twice as hard as before.

The little band played long into the evening, but the princess didn't laugh. Jack began to worry that he would spend the rest of his life chained in a dungeon. The tiny animals were all so tired that the bee stopped strumming, and the exhausted mouse fell panting to the floor. Suddenly, the grasshopper leapt to the throne, stood in front of the princess and began to sing.

Never in her royal life had the princess laughed so hard, and never had Jack been so relieved. He dropped to his knees, "My lady, I have won you for my own."

THE GRASSHOPPER, THE MOUSE, THE BEE, AND THE HARP

Jack was washed, dressed in silk and gold, and presented to the princess. Naturally, they fell in love on the spot. The wedding lasted ten days and ten nights. When it was over, Jack's mother was happy, sadness disappeared from the kingdom, and laughter filled the land. And the bee, the mouse and the grasshopper retired to a quiet garden.

And what of the mysterious man at the fair? On misty nights under a full moon, he is often seen dancing in the meadow with three cows. ■

THE HEDGEHOG

The spring air was fresh and cool from the rain. Hedgehog was on her way home to her burrow after a pleasant evening in the countryside. She had managed to get a drink of warm milk from a cow sleeping in the field. She had even rolled in a pile of crabapples and speared a few on her sharp spines to take home. "Who else would dare such things?" she wondered proudly.

And who else could curl up into a tight, prickly ball to protect herself from danger? She looked around cautiously for signs of the fox.

The grass was damp and sweet as she scuttled along. Up ahead the river otter was at play again.

HEDGEHOG

Imitating others' behavior can often have negative results. This little tale, adapted from British folklore about the endearing little hedgehog, illustrates that each of us is unique for a reason, and should be admired for our own special qualities.

THE HEDGEHOG

She loved to watch him—he was so sleek and graceful as he pranced up the hill. She sighed with envy as he threw himself from the top of the soft, wet hill and with feet and legs pointed backward, slid all the way down like a streamlined, fur-covered missile.

"Oh, I *must* do that," said Hedgehog. "It looks so easy." Up the hill she climbed, lumpy with apples and sticky with spines, picking up bits of grass and mud as she went.

The otter saw her and worried that she would hurt herself. "I don't think you should try that," he warned. "You're not built for it. And look out for the fox before you leap!"

It was too late. The hedgehog had already flung herself on her round little stomach, and was rolling forward topsy-turvy down the hill, becoming a giant ball of grass and mud. Picking up speed, she hurtled headlong toward the fox's den, where he lay dreaming of tasty, hedgehog stew.

Faster and faster the hedgehog rolled, right into the den and right into the fox. He sprang to his feet and growled. What was this peculiar thing that woke him from a sound sleep and stuck like thorns? He sniffed it carefully. What a strange concoction of spikes, mud, grass, and . . . "What's this? Apples?" He pulled them out and ate them. The he pushed and rolled the offensive prickly thing out of his den, and went back to sleep.

The terrified hedgehog shook off most of the mess and waddled as fast as she could back to her burrow, where she thought about her close call. "I'm not built to slide down hills like the otter. I'm lucky all I lost were the apples." Then she curled into a tight little ball. "The otter can't do this. Neither can the fox," she chuckled, and went to sleep.

After that spine-raising experience, Hedgehog was content just to watch the lovely otter's downhill flights. ▪

RAT AND THE CHINESE ZODIAC

Long ago and far away in China, the Emperor of All Things sat in his lotus garden. He looked at the 12-year calendar and all its confusing symbols, and shook his head. He called his Prime Minister. "What year is this?" he asked.

"I am not sure, your excellency. First, I will have to study the calendar and the almanac and our zodiac, and then consult with the Royal Council," the Prime Minister said, bowing.

"No one understands this confusing calendar, least of all me, and I am the Emperor. We must get rid of all these symbols and give each year a new and simple name." Then the Emperor smiled and clapped his hands. "I have it," he said. "The *zo* in zodiac means animal. We will name each of the twelve calendar years after an animal!"

RAT

The Chinese zodiac, or calendar, is divided into 12-year cycles. Each year is named after an animal. The word *zodiac* literally means a circle of animals. This legend about how the first year was named after small Rat instead of big, strong Ox illustrates that cleverness and wisdom are not a matter of size.

RAT AND THE CHINESE ZODIAC

The Prime Minister was surprised. "But which animals?"

"We will invite all the animals in China to a great feast, and then we will decide," the Emperor proclaimed. "Buddha will be pleased."

When word went out to the kingdom that twelve animals had accepted the Emperor's invitation, preparations were made for the celebration. Food was cooked, bright lanterns were hung, and delicate music filled the air.

The Emperor sat on his jade throne, wearing his finest silk robes. Oh, what excitement there would be in the palace and the village!

"The animals have arrived," the Prime Minister announced. One by one, twelve animals came and stood before the throne. They bowed respectfully. "We are honored to be here. Thank you for your kindness," they said.

"You have honored me with your presence," the Emperor said kindly. "I wish to name each of the twelve years in our calendar after an animal. Since there are twelve of you here, each year will be named for one of you."

Suddenly, a small, brown rat stepped timidly forward. "Which animal will be first, oh Wise One? I am clever and smart—could I lead the first year?"

The great Ox spoke out. "But I am big and very strong. Surely I should be first for such an important year."

The Emperor had not thought about the first year one way or another. So he asked the animals who they would choose, and immediately they began to argue, taking sides and behaving poorly.

"Stop this at once," commanded the Emperor. "We will let the people of the kingdom decide." He ordered the Prime Minister to go with the animals and ask everyone who should be first.

The people seemed to favor Ox, and paid no attention to Rat. "How can anything so small be clever and wise?" they asked.

Naturally, Rat became upset. "No one notices me next to Ox," he said to the Prime Minister. "How can I become as big?"

"Importance is not a matter of size. You must *believe* you are big enough to do the job," he answered.

Rat did as he was asked. He closed his eyes and thought about the special things that rats could do. They were certainly clever and brave—hadn't his cousin freed a lion from its trap? He imagined himself as big as a rabbit, a capybara, an ox, as big as . . . *himself.*

RAT AND THE CHINESE ZODIAC

Then he went out into the village. He stood tall and held his tail high and walked proudly. Children stared and pointed in disbelief at Rat and forgot all about Ox.

Everyone talked about Rat. "Ox is strong and hard working. But Rat is clever, ambitious and probably wise. Look how confident he is."

The Emperor was quite surprised by the whole event. "A rat that can convince the entire kingdom he's as big as the ox must be special indeed, and want this job very much. Therefore, Rat will lead the first year, and Ox the second. Let our celebration begin."

The animals followed the Emperor in the order they would rule the twelve years of the calendar: Rat, Ox, Tiger, Rabbit, Dragon, Snake, Horse, Sheep, Monkey, Rooster, Dog, and Pig. The Emperor was happy because now he would always know what year it was.

And Rat? He led the first year with wisdom and justice. And as Ox often observed, "You don't have to be big to be smart, for true greatness comes from the heart." ▪

THE EAGLE AND THE SHRIKE

A long time ago, when animals ruled the Earth, there were often contests among them about who was strongest, wisest, or biggest.

One day, the birds began to argue noisily about which of them could fly the highest. Some said it was clever Hawk who flew with great speed. Others were absolutely certain it was mighty Eagle with his incredible strength and power.

But to their amazement, the little gray Shrike, no bigger than a pigeon, announced that he could fly higher than any bird, including Eagle and Hawk. "That would be very easy," he boasted, insulting all of birdom. Insults flew back and forth. Eagle and Hawk watched quietly as the birds squawked and chirped and screamed and hummed, flapping their wings and puffing their feathers.

THE EAGLE AND THE SHRIKE

Finally, Great Horned Owl grew tired of the endless bickering that had kept him awake all day. It was time to settle this matter once and for all. "Tomorrow there will be a contest to decide who flies highest. As the oldest and wisest among you, *I* will judge."

The following day, all the People of the Sky flocked together for the big event—Mockingbird and Osprey, Dove, Sparrow and Goose, Raven, Duck, Swan and Robin, Eagle and Hawk. Every bird wanted to see who could fly the highest. When Owl gave three, loud whoo-whoo-hoots, the contest began. With whirring and flurries and beating of wings, the birds took to the sky.

The hawk flew at incredible speed, flying straight up and dropping straight down. But Eagle rode on a strong current of air and rose higher and higher. His great wings carried him far above the Earth as he soared toward the sun.

But where was Shrike? Unknown to the others, he had hidden himself on Eagle's back, tucked out of sight between the wings. How clever he was! Who would notice that he had hitched a ride? And what did it matter anyway, as long as he won?

As Eagle navigated the wind, Shrike stood unsteadily on his feet and shrieked, "I am highest! I am highest!" He flapped his wings and pretended to fly alone.

Hearing this, the great eagle folded his wings and dropped quickly back to Earth. Above him the shrike flew down as well. "Here I am," he announced in his shrill voice. "Tell the Feathered Tribes that I am ruler of the air."

How could this be? The birds all waited breathlessly as Great Horned Owl spoke. "The winner of this contest has flown higher, farther and closer to the sun than any of you."

Shrike puffed and preened and strutted.

"Not only has the winner *flown* highest," continued Owl, "he has also carried an extra weight on his back—the shrike who could not fly as high. Only one of us has such strength and power. Mighty Eagle, ruler of the sky."

He turned to Shrike who suddenly looked very small. "You tried to deceive your friends and bring dishonor to Eagle. You cheated to win! You are no longer one of us. From now on, you will fly no higher than the trees, and the black mask you wear will remind everyone of your deception."

All the birds then rose up in a great cloud and moved across the sky. Above them all soared Eagle. ▲

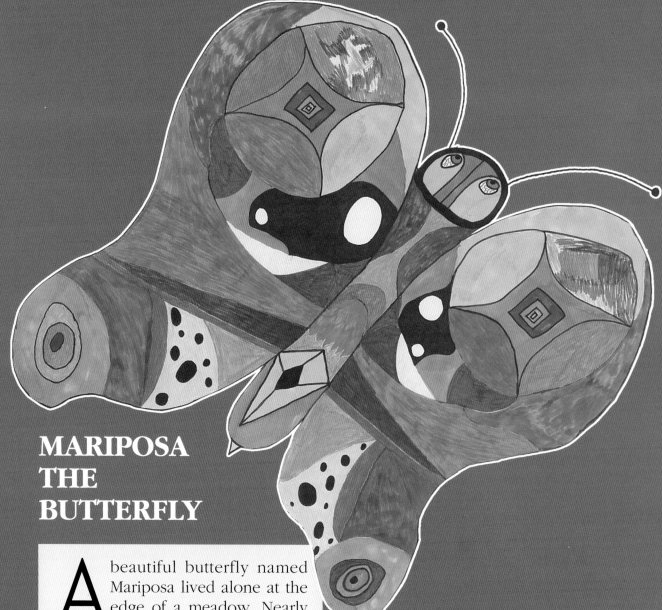

MARIPOSA
THE
BUTTERFLY

A beautiful butterfly named Mariposa lived alone at the edge of a meadow. Nearly every day, a parade of animals came by to gaze at her. They all wanted to marry her but none could win her heart. Mariposa loved music and none of them could sing.

One morning she heard singing in the grass nearby. The song tinkled like bluebells and danced like raindrops. She flew here and

BUTTERFLY

A butterfly learns that life has problems but nothing is insurmountable in this simple, traditional tale from Mexico about love, loss, sadness and renewal.

there and found it was a little mouse. He told her he loved flowers so much he spent his days singing to them. Mariposa was enchanted and lost her heart to him.

"I can't offer you much, O Fragile Beauty," said Mouse. "All I have are songs, whiskers, a long tail—and so much love."

"And I have only bright colors, two wings—and so much love, my charming mouse," she answered.

And so they were married and spent their days visiting all the flowers in the meadow. But now, the mouse sang only for his beloved Mariposa. While he sang, she mixed new colors for the flowers by taking a little from here and putting it there. They were very happy.

One day, Mouse went on a seed-gathering trip and never came back. Mariposa waited and waited. She neither slept nor ate, and when she saw a cat lurking nearby, she knew what had happened to her dear Mouse.

Her heart was broken. She stopped visiting the flowers because they reminded her too much of her lost love. Without nectar, her colors faded and her wings were pale. Without her, the flowers began to fade, too.

She was surprised one afternoon when her friend the bird, Pajaro Cú, came to see her. "I came to tell you that we are all worried about you," sang Cú. "You look terrible, and so do the flowers. You're their only hope."

Mariposa fluttered softly. She looked up and saw the flowers were almost gone. Oh, what would little Mouse have thought! "I can't live without him," she whispered.

"Yes, you can," sang Pajaro Cú. "Love doesn't die when you pass it on."

And so she did. From flower, to flower, to flower. ▲

THE BUZZARD AND THE DOVE

The big buzzard was tired. He had worked hard all day circling the air and sitting on clifftops, looking for rotten things to eat. It was a dirty job but it was *his* job, and he was proud of it. Now, one last time before sunset, he trudged to the cliff's edge, spread his wings and jumped off.

Warm air currents lifted him up and he soared like a huge, black kite, his wings straight and unmoving. His eyes searched for dead animals that littered the landscape below. There was plenty that needed cleaning up down there, but he just wasn't hungry.

He had not been hungry since he first set eyes on the beautiful

THE BUZZARD AND THE DOVE

Dove. She was so delicate, so lovely, and her song was so sweet. He could think of nothing else but her. Finally, he decided to tell her how he felt before he died of love or starved to death.

First, he made himself presentable. He wiped his head and beak in the grass, splashed in a shallow pond, and cleaned and rearranged his feathers. In the reflecting water he saw his naked pink head and heavy beak, and the fluffed, ruffled collar around his rubbery neck. He was ready! Off he waddled on huge clawed feet in search of his true love.

He saw her, small and perfect, on the branch of a tulip tree. Oh, her tiny beak, her creamy feathers, her little toes. He fixed his eyes on his love, and could hardly speak. "Oh, divine Dove, princess of the sky, I have loved you from afar and humbly ask for your wing in marriage."

The dove looked at him as though seeing a nightmare. "What? Are you crazy? You ugly bird, do you know what you look like? Get away from me this instant!"

The buzzard, though not handsome, was very polite, and with great courtesy he spoke to her. "Please look beyond my appearance. The feathers I wear are not beautiful colors, but they are suited to the work I do. And my feet are big for the very same reason. But you, lovely angel, have nothing to do but decorate the trees. I have made a terrible mistake in thinking you could love me."

The buzzard went away, sad, hopeless and very embarrassed. Time passed, but he could not stop thinking of the dove. "I gave up too easily," he thought. "I must try again." So he preened and washed and scrubbed and combed, and imagined that his feathers were a rainbow of colors. He tried walking without a waddle, and went in search of his dove.

He found her in a pomegranate tree, nibbling its fruit. "Forgive me again," he said awkwardly, "but would you at least give me your friendship? I will fly you higher than you have ever been and show you a world you have never seen."

The vain, proud dove was cold as ice. "You're back again? Buzz off, Buzzard. I don't love you. I don't even like you. The smell from your beak is disgusting, and the way you walk is awful. And those legs!" Oh, she was vicious.

But, as always, Buzzard was polite. "Why can't you look at my courage

39

THE BUZZARD AND THE DOVE

and respect what I do? I and my kind keep the fields and roads clean so that you don't have to. I had no idea you were as heartless as you are."

The dove continued to list his faults. Then, dismissing him entirely, she flew to the top of the tree and began to coo. The poor buzzard's heart was broken. He lifted himself slowly and heavily into the air, and floated into a watermelon sky.

Long, lonely days passed. Then one morning, he noticed other buzzards flying by his perch. "Hey, Buzz," one of them called out. "There's work to do and we need you." The buzzard snapped to attention. His job! He had almost forgotten how important it was. It was time to get back to it.

He waddled to the cliff's edge, caught a wind current, and remembered something important. "I am no dove. She was. She was no buzzard, but I am." He looked down on the landscape below and his appetite came back. ▲

TWO BIRDS
Adapted from an Eastern
European fable about
stubbornness.

TWO BIRDS

Two very colorful but solitary birds lived on opposite sides of a river. On one side grew bushes heavy with ripe raspberries and trees with red apples. On the other side, the ground was covered with sweet wild strawberries the size of peas, and violets with centers like sugar.

Each bird often crossed the log in the middle of the river to sample the offerings on the other side. One day, they both happened to cross at the same time, and met in the middle. "Please back up and let me pass," said the raspberry bird with bushy feathers.

"Back up, yourself," said the other. "I was here first." The corners of his big beak turned down and the three feathers on his head stood up.

"What? You're in my way. Get off my log," said Bushy Bird.

TWO BIRDS

"Your log? Move, please. I'm crossing over," ordered Big Beak.

And so they argued for hours. They puffed, preened and flapped their wings, squawked, chirped and screamed at each other until their feathers were in complete disarray. Neither one would back up, so neither one could move forward.

They stood there, beak to beak, in angry silence. Soon, Bushy Bird began to smile. "You should see yourself," he said with sarcasm. "How stubborn you look."

That was the last straw for Big Beak. In the fray, both birds fell off the log and into the water. Soaked and furious, they struggled back to their own side of the river and pulled themselves ashore. While they dried out and cooled down, they thought about the tasty fruit they didn't get.

If only one of them had backed up, they both could have crossed the river. The next time, that's just what they did. ▲

OWL

A wise old owl sat in an oak.
The more he saw, the less he spoke.
The less he spoke, the more he heard.
Why can't we all be like that wise old bird?

Anon.

Bibliography

Aarne, Antti. Amatus. The Types of the Folktale: A Classification and Bibliography. Helsinki: Academia Scientarum Fennica, 1913 (?).

Aesop's Fables (English and Greek). The Medici Aesop: Spencer MS 50 from the Spencer Collection of the N.Y. Public Library. Translated by Bernard McTique. New York: Abrams, 1989. (Piero de'Medici, 1416-1469.)

Arnott, Kathleen. Animal Folk Tales Around the World. New York: Henry Z.Walck, 1970.

Aymar, Brandt, ed. The Personality of the Bird. New York: Crown, 1965.

Barbosa, Rogerio Andrade. African Animal Tales. Volcano, CA: Volcano Press, 1993.

Beard, Peter. Longing for Darkness: Kamante's Tales from Out of Africa. New York: Harcourt Brace Jovanovich, 1975.

Bierhorst, John. Black Rainbow: Legends of Myths of Ancient Peru. New York: Farrar, Straus & Giroux, 1976.

Bilibin, Ivan I. Trans. by Robert Chandler. Russian Folk Tales. Boulder, CO: Shambala and New York: Random House, 1980.

Bobbit, Ellen C. Jataka Tales Retold. New York: The Century Co., 1912.

Bowes, Anne La Bastille. Bird Kingdom of the Mayas. Princeton, NJ: Van Nostrand, 1967.

Climo, Shirley. Someone Saw a Spider: Spider Facts & Folktales. New York: Crowell, 1985.

Cook, Joseph. Curious World of the Crab. New York: Dodd Mead, 1970.

Colum, Padraic. Legends of Hawaii. New Haven, CT: Yale University Press, 1937.

Courlander, Harold. A Treasury of African Folklore. New York, Crown, 1975.

Cousteau, Jacques-Yves. The Shark: Splendid Savage of the Sea. New York: A & W Publishers, 1970.

Davidson, Margaret. Nine True Dolphin Stories. New York: Scholastic, 1974.

DeRoin, Nancy. Jataka Tales: Fables from the Buddha. Boston: Houghton Mifflin, 1975.

Devine, Eleanore and Martha Clark. The Dolphin Smile: Twenty-nine Centuries of Dolphin Lore. New York: Macmillan, 1967.

Eberhard, Wolfram. Folktales of China. Toronto: University of Toronto Press, 1965.

Encyclopedia Britannica. Entry on Arion, Vol. 1, p. 552.

_____. Entry on Periander, Vol. 9, p. 289.

_____. Entry on Robert I (the Bruce), Vol. 11, p. 104.

Faulkner, William. The Days When Animals Talked: Black American Folk Tales. Chicago: Follet, 1977.

Gambell, Roy. The Concise Illustrated Book of Whales and Dolphins. New York: Smithmark, 1991.

Glueck, Nelson. Deities and Dolphins. New York: Farrar Straus & Giroux, 1965.

Greaves, Nick. When Hippo Was Hairy and Other Tales From Africa. New York: Barron's, 1988.

Guterman, Norbert. Russian Fairy Tales. New York: Pantheon/Random House, 1973.

Hayes, Joe. Mariposa Mariposa. Santa Fe, NM: Trails West, 1988.

Jones, V. S. Vernon. Aesop's Fables: A New Translation. New York: Doubleday, Page, 1912.

Koch, Kenneth and Kate Farrell. Talking to the Sun: An Illustrated Anthology of Poems for Young People. New York: Metropolitan Museum of Art and Holt Rinehart & Winston, 1985.

Krutch, Joseph. A Treasury of Birdlore. New York, Doubleday, 1962.

La Fontaine, Jean. The Fables of La Fontaine - 1621-1695. New York: Viking, 1954.

L'Estrange, Sir Roger. Fables of Aesop According to Sir Roger L'Estrange. New York: Dover, 1967.

Lavine, Sigmund A. Wonders of Rhinos. New York: Dodd Mead, 1982.

McManus, Seumas. Donegal Fairy Stories. New York: Doubleday-Doran, 1900.

MacDonald, Margaret Read. Peace Tales: World Folktales to Talk About. Hamden, CT: Linnet Books, 1992.

_____. The Storyteller's Sourcebook: A Subject, Title & Motif Index to Folklore Collections for Children. Detroit, MI: Neal-Schuman, 1982.

Montejo, Victor. The Bird Who Cleans the World, and Other Mayan Fables. Willimantic, CT: Curbstone, 1991.

Newcomb, Franc Johnson. Navaho Folk Tales. Muscum of Navaho Ceremonial Art, 1967.

Pryor, Karen and Kenneth Norris. Dolphin Societies: Discoveries and Puzzles. Berkeley: Univ. of California Press, 1991.

Saxe, John Godfrey. "The Blind Men and the Elephant." In The Poetical Works of John Godfrey Saxe. Boston & NY: Houghton Mifflin, 1882.

Scott, Ronald McNair. Robert the Bruce, King of Scots. New York: P. Bedrick Books, 1989.

Shah, Idries. World Tales. New York: Harcourt Brace Jovanovich, 1979.

Spector, Norman B. Complete Fables of Jean de La Fontaine. Evanston, IL: Northwestern University Press, 1988.

Spinage, C. A. The Book of the Giraffe. Boston: Houghton Mifflin, 1968.

Thompson, Stith. Motif-Index of Folk Literature: A Classification of Narrative Elements in Folktales, Ballads, Myth, Fables, Medieval, Exempla, Fabliaux, Jest-Books and Local Legends. Bloomington: Univ. of Indiana Press, 1955-58 (6 vols.).

_____. One Hundred Favorite Folktales. Bloomington: Univ. of Indiana Press, 1968.

Tibbits, Alison, and Alan Roocroft. California Condors. Mankato, MN: Capstone Press, 1992.

Walters, Derek. Chinese Mythology: An Encyclopedia of Myths and Legends. London: Aquarian/Thorsons, 1992.

Weinstein, Krystyna. The Owl in Art, Myth, and Legend. New York: Crescent Books, 1989.

Whitney, Alex. Stiff Ears: Animal Folktales of the North American Indian. New York: H.Z. Walck, 1974.

Wooton, Anthony. Animal Folklore, Myth and Legend. United Kingdom: Blandford Press, 1968.

Published in the United States by
Roberts Rinehart Publishers
P.O. Box 666, Niwot, Colorado 80544

Published in Ireland by
Roberts Rinehart Publishers
Trinity House, Charleston Road
Ranelaigh, Dublin 6

ISBN 1-57098-003-9
Library of Congress Catalog Card Number 94-66096

Distributed in the United States and Canada by
Publishers Group West

Designed by Jody Chapel, Cover to Cover Design
Printed in Mexico